Titles in Series S852

Cinderella

Three Little Pigs

Goldilocks and the Three Bears

Jack and the beanstalk

Snow White and the Seven Dwarfs

The Ugly Duckling

Sleeping Beauty

Hansel and Gretel

The Gingerbread Man

Red Riding Hood

These titles are also available in two gift box sets

British Library Cataloguing in Publication Data

Randall, Ronne
The gingerbread man. — (First fairy tales)
I. Title   II. Burton, Terry   III. Series
813'.54[J]   PZ7
ISBN 0-7214-9560-5

First edition

Published by Ladybird Books Ltd Loughborough Leicestershire UK
Ladybird Books Inc Lewiston Maine 04240 USA
© LADYBIRD BOOKS LTD MCMLXXXVII

Printed in England

The Gingerbread Man

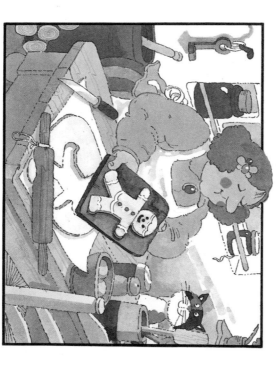

written by RONNE RANDALL
illustrated by TERRY BURTON

Ladybird Books

Once upon a time, there was a little old woman and a little old man. They lived together in a little old house by the side of the road.

One day, the little old woman said, "I will make something special for tea today. I will make a little gingerbread man."

So the little old woman made the gingerbread. She cut out a head, and a body, and legs for the gingerbread man. She made his coat out of sugar, with currant buttons. She made his face out of raisins.

Then she popped the gingerbread man in the oven to bake.

Soon the little old man came home for tea.

"Something smells good!" he said to the little old woman.

"It is the gingerbread man, baking in the oven," she said. "I'll just have a look and see if he's ready." She opened the oven door and the gingerbread man jumped right out!

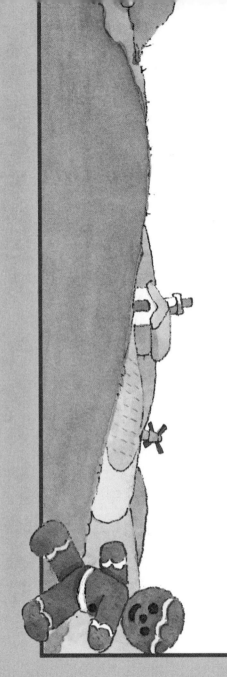

The gingerbread man ran across the kitchen floor. "Stop!" "Stop!" cried the little old woman.

"Stop!" cried the little old man.

But the gingerbread man did not stop. He ran out of the door and straight down the road. As he ran, he sang:

"Run, run, as fast as you can.
You can't catch me, I'm the gingerbread man!"

The little old woman and the little old man ran after him.

The gingerbread man ran past a big, grey cat sitting on a fence.

"Stop!" called the cat. "You look good enough to eat, and I'm hungry."

But the gingerbread man did not stop. He ran faster, and as he ran, he sang:

"Run, run, as fast as you can.
You can't catch me, I'm the gingerbread man!
I've run away from a little old man,
and a little old woman,
And I can run away from you, I can!"

The cat jumped off the fence and ran after the gingerbread man.

The gingerbread man ran past a brown dog lying beside a hedge.

"Stop!" called the dog. "You look good enough to eat, and I'm hungry!"

But the gingerbread man did not stop. He ran faster, and as he ran, he sang:

"Run, run, as fast as you can.
You can't catch me, I'm the gingerbread man!
I've run away from a cat, a little old woman,
and a little old man,
And I can run away from you, I can!"

The dog stood up and ran after the gingerbread man.

The gingerbread man ran past a cow in a field.

"Stop!" called the cow. "You look good enough to eat, and I'm tired of all this grass!"

But the gingerbread man did not stop. He ran faster, and as he ran, he sang:

"Run, run, as fast as you can.
You can't catch me, I'm the gingerbread man!
I've run away from a dog, a cat,
a little old woman, and a little old man,
And I can run away from you, I can!"

The cow left the field and ran after the gingerbread man.

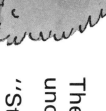

The gingerbread man ran past a fox sitting under a tree by the river.

"Stop!" said the fox. "I want to talk to you."

But the gingerbread man did not stop. He ran faster, and as he ran, he sang:

"Run, run, as fast as you can.
You can't catch me, I'm the gingerbread man!
I've run away from a cow, a dog, a cat,
a little old woman, and a little old man,
And I can run away from you, I can!"

The sly fox just smiled.

The gingerbread man came to the river.
He could not swim.

"How can I get across?" he asked the fox.
"I will help you," said the fox.
"Jump onto my tail."

The gingerbread man jumped onto the fox's tail. The fox began to swim across the river.

Soon the fox said, "The water is getting deeper. Jump onto my back so you won't get wet."

The gingerbread man jumped onto the fox's back.

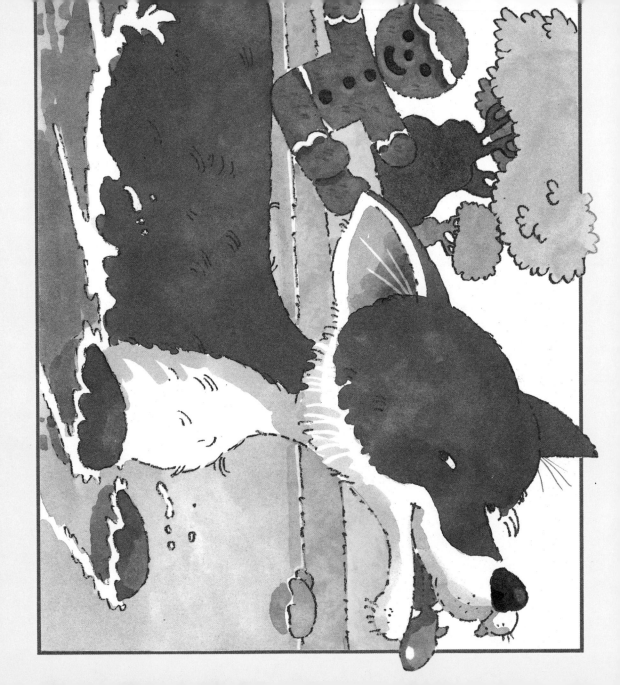

The fox kept on swimming. Soon he said, "The water is getting even deeper. Jump onto my head, so you won't get wet."

The gingerbread man jumped onto the fox's head.

The fox kept on swimming. Soon he said, "The water is getting *very* deep! Jump onto my nose so you won't get wet."

The gingerbread man jumped onto the fox's nose.

Quick as a wink, the fox opened his mouth and gobbled up the gingerbread man.

And that was the end of the little gingerbread man!